SHERWOOD WALKS HOME

SHERWOOD WALKS HOME

STORY AND PICTURES BY
JAMES FLORA

HARCOURT, BRACE & WORLD, INC.
NEW YORK

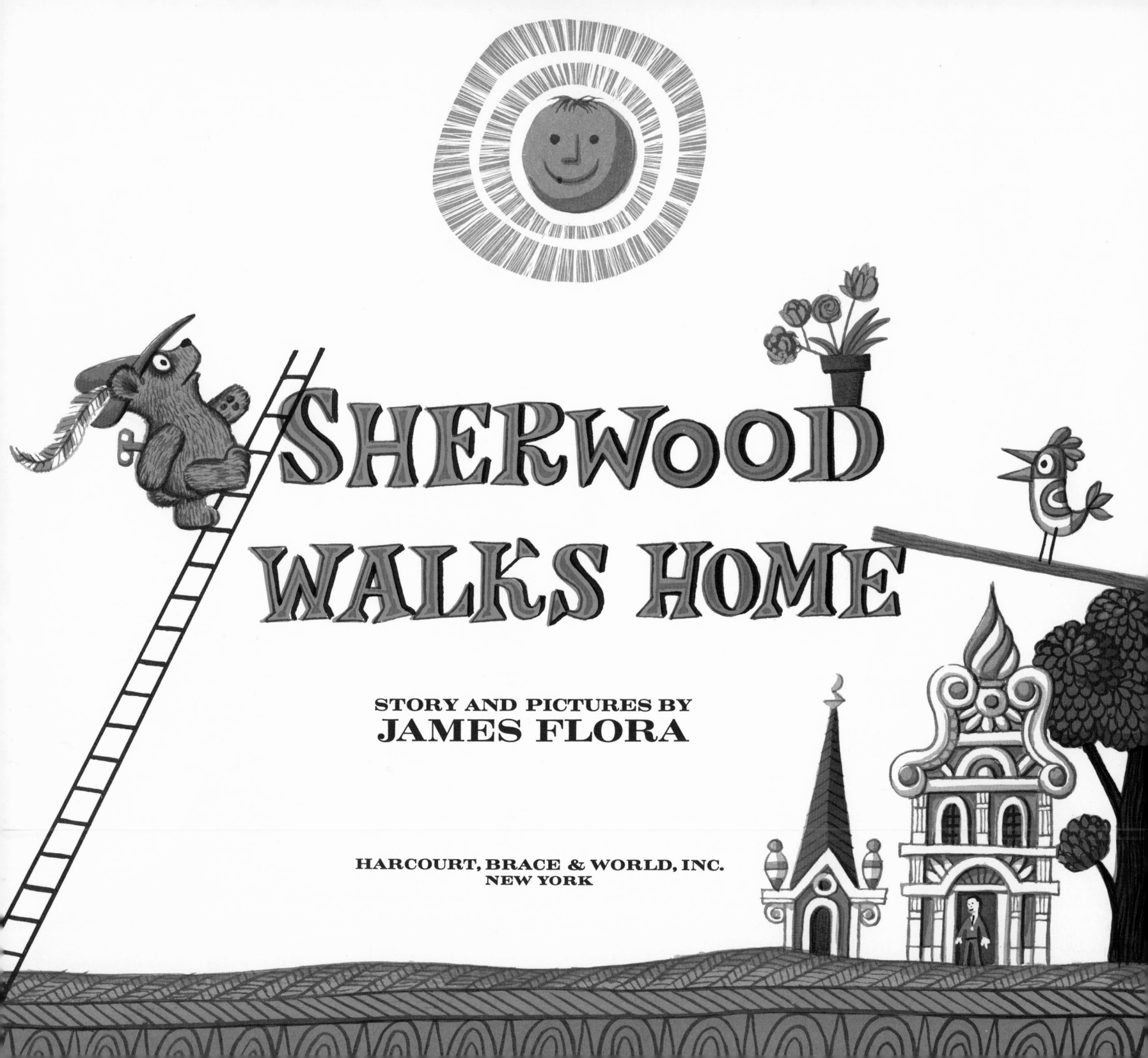

FOR JANE
who makes a fine home
for all of us Floras

When it started to rain in the park, Robert ran home. He didn't want to get his new suit wet. He was in such a hurry that he forgot Sherwood.

Sherwood sat there all alone in the rain. Water dripped off of his hat onto his nose. Sherwood couldn't run home because he is a wind-up bear and there was nobody to wind him up.

All night long Sherwood sat in the park. It was cold and wet and lonely. Once, in the middle of the night, he saw two eyes staring at him.

"Please come and wind me so I can walk home," Sherwood begged. But the eyes just blinked and disappeared.

Sherwood never did see who owned them.

In the morning the rain stopped and the sun peeked through the trees. Sherwood felt much better.

"It won't be long until someone will come and wind me up," he said to himself. And sure enough someone did.

A man passed and saw Sherwood. He picked him up and wiped him dry.

"What a nice fuzzy wind-up bear," the man said. "I'll wind him up and take him home to my boy George."

As soon as Sherwood felt all wound up, he jumped to the ground and ran for home.

"STOP!" shouted the man. "Come back and be my bear."

"I can't be your bear," said Sherwood. "I am Robert's bear, and I'm going home to him now."

He ran through the park until he came to the zoo. Sherwood didn't want to go to the zoo, but he had to. Wind-up bears can't turn corners or walk around things. They have to walk straight ahead. So Sherwood walked through the zoo and right into the bear's cage. The big Mama Bear grabbed him.

"Oooh! What a lovely bear," she said. "You are going to be my baby bear."

"I can't be your baby bear," said Sherwood. "I'm Robert's bear, and I must go home before my motor runs down."

But the Mama Bear wouldn't listen to that. She hugged Sherwood until his springs creaked. She licked his fur until he looked like new. Then she made him eat some bear food. Sherwood hoped it wouldn't gum up his motor.

Finally the Mama Bear lay down for her nap. As soon as she was fast asleep, Sherwood hopped out of her arms and ran out of the cage.

He walked through the park until he came to a big lake. He couldn't walk around it. He had to walk straight in.

People in boats looked down and saw a bear walking on the bottom. They were so surprised that they dropped their oars.

Fish were so surprised to see a bear under the water that they swam right out of the lake. All except one fish.

"Yum-yum," the fish said. "I've been looking for something nice for lunch, and here comes a tasty bear."

"I can't be your lunch," said Sherwood. "I'm Robert's bear, and I must get home before my motor unwinds."

The fish chased after him. He caught Sherwood by his tail and wouldn't let go.

So Sherwood walked out of the lake dragging the fish behind him.

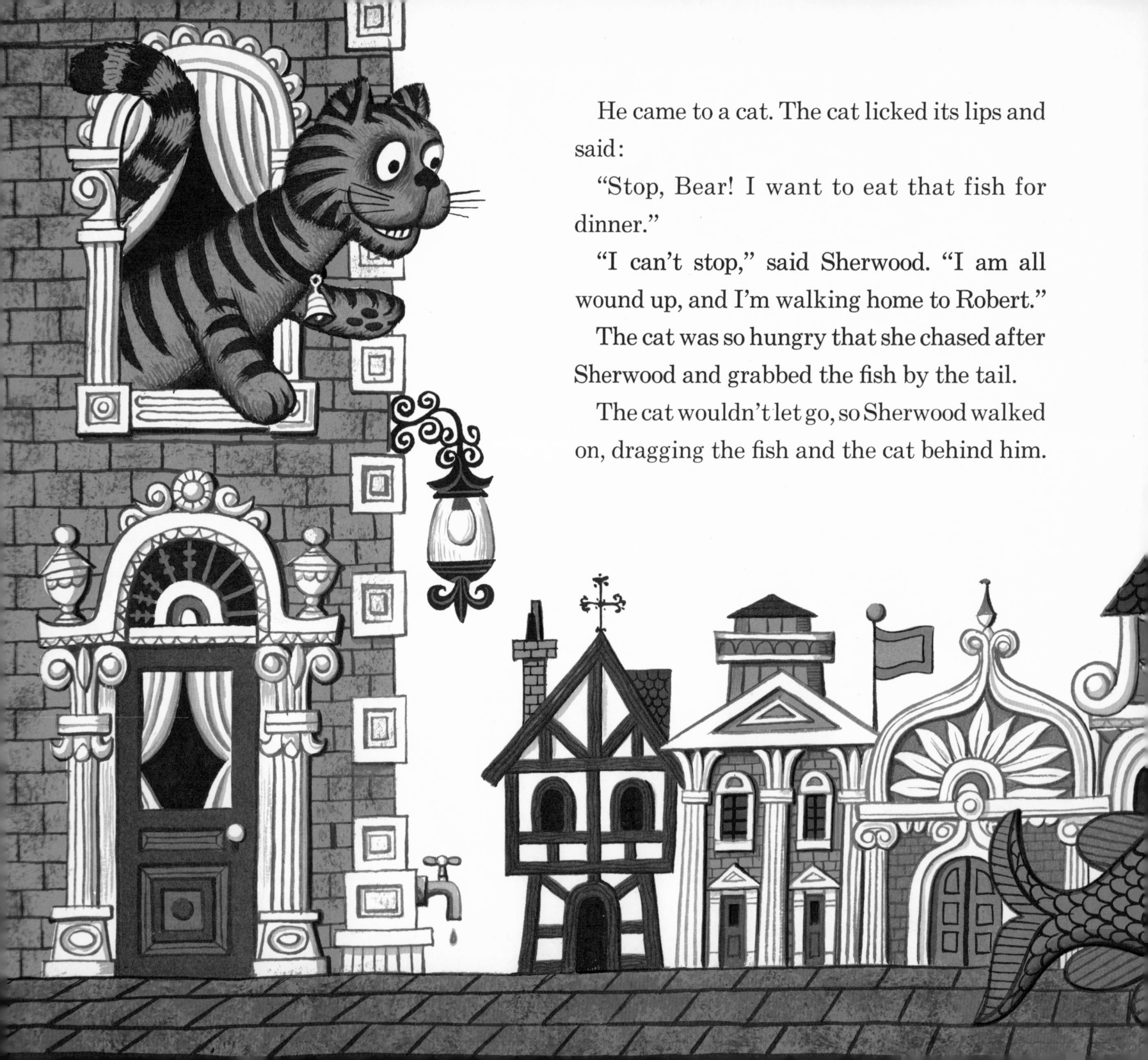

He came to a cat. The cat licked its lips and said:

"Stop, Bear! I want to eat that fish for dinner."

"I can't stop," said Sherwood. "I am all wound up, and I'm walking home to Robert."

The cat was so hungry that she chased after Sherwood and grabbed the fish by the tail.

The cat wouldn't let go, so Sherwood walked on, dragging the fish and the cat behind him.

They came to a big dog chewing on a bone.

"Stop, Bear!" said the dog. "I want to chase your cat."

"I can't stop," said Sherwood. "I am all wound up, and I am walking home to Robert."

But the dog didn't believe that. He chased after them and grabbed the cat by the tail. He wouldn't let go. So Sherwood walked on, dragging the fish and the cat and the dog behind him.

They came to a little girl with a leash in her hand. She ran after the dog and fastened it to his collar.

"You naughty dog. You shouldn't run away," she said. "Stop, Bear! I want to take my dog home."

"I can't stop," said Sherwood. "I must go home to Robert before my motor runs down."

But the little girl wouldn't let go, so Sherwood walked on dragging the fish, the cat, the dog, and the little girl behind him.

They came to a street full of cars. All of the cars screeched to a stop and blew their horns. A big policeman shouted:

"STOP! You can't cross the street on a red light. It's against the law."

"We can't stop," said the little girl. "My dog won't let go of the cat. The cat won't let go of the fish, and the fish won't let go of the bear."

"And I can't stop," said Sherwood, "because I have to get home to Robert before my motor runs down."

The policeman took the little girl's hand and pulled and pulled, but he couldn't pull her loose. So Sherwood walked on with the fish, the cat, the dog, the girl, and the policeman trailing behind him.

They came to a big parade. Sherwood crossed in front of it.

"STOP!" shouted the drum major with the gold braid and silver buttons. "Get out of the way. Can't you see you're stopping the parade?"

"We can't stop," said the policeman. "Nobody will let go. Lend me a hand and help me pull them apart."

So the big drum major grabbed the policeman's hand and pulled and pulled and pulled. But nobody would let go. So Sherwood walked on down the street pulling them all behind him.

Wherever a drum major goes, the band is sure to follow. Down the street they all marched. Sherwood led the parade, and after him came the fish, the cat, the dog, the girl, the policeman, the drum major, and all the drums and horns and crashing cymbals.

It was a beautiful parade, and everybody stopped to look and listen. But Sherwood was worried. He could feel his motor running down. He was walking slower and slower. He knew that if he stopped, the fish would swallow him and he never would get home to Robert.

MARCH—MARch—March—march. Each step was slower than the one before.

He could see his house. If only he could get through the door and up the stairs, then Robert would save him.

Slower and slower he walked. Now he was through the door and going up the stairs. Would he ever get to the top? He could hear his motor grinding inside him.

"Click-rr-r—click-a-tick—rr—r!"

It was almost run down.

ALBERT

Now he had reached the top of the
stairs. Just as he opened the door to
Robert's room, *his motor stopped*.

He couldn't move.

He couldn't even turn his head to see
if the fish was going to gobble him up.

But Robert saw it. Quick as a flash he grabbed Sherwood. He pulled him away just as the fish's jaws snapped shut.

Then with a gulp the cat swallowed the fish and ran away. The dog chased after the cat and so did the girl and the policeman and the drum major and all of the band. They tumbled down the stairs and out into the street with horns blowing, drums beating, and cymbals crashing.

But Sherwood didn't care. He had walked home before his motor had run down. He hadn't been swallowed! He was home at last and Robert was hugging him, and hugging is what Sherwood likes better than anything.

He was so happy and so tired that he fell asleep with his hat on—which is something that nobody should do.

Not even wind-up bears with sore tails.

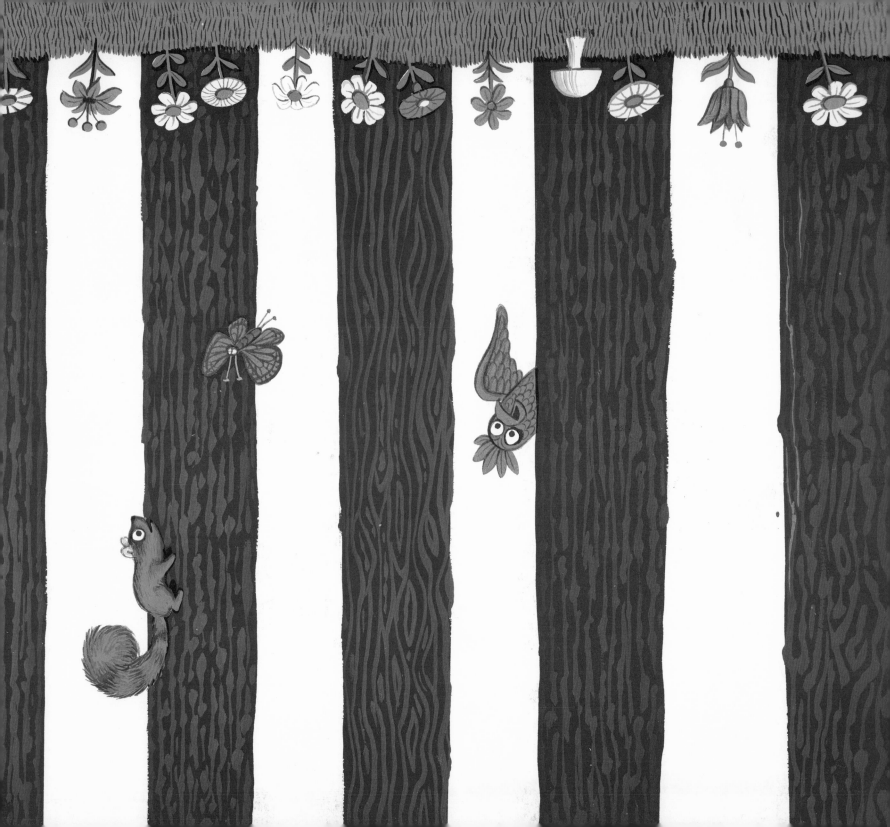